BUGLETTE
the messy sleeper

by bethanie deeney murguia

TRICYCLE PRESS
Berkeley

For Adam and my favorite little bugs, Ana and Audrey
—B.D.M.

The author would like to thank Amy Novesky and Mary Kole for their guidance.

All rights reserved. Published in the United States by Tricycle Press, an imprint
of Random House Children's Books, a division of Random House, Inc., New York.
www.randomhouse.com/kids

Tricycle Press and the Tricycle Press colophon are registered trademarks of Random House, Inc.

Library of Congress Cataloging-in-Publication Data
Murguia, Bethanie Deeney.
Buglette the messy sleeper / by Bethanie Deeney Murguia. — 1st ed.
p. cm.
Summary: A little bug has big adventures while she sleeps, but her mother worries
that her thrashing about will create problems for the family.
[1. Sleep—Fiction. 2. Dreams—Fiction. 3. Insects—Fiction.] I. Title.
PZ7.M944Bu 2011
[E]—dc22
2010009015

ISBN 978-1-58246-375-9 (hardcover)
ISBN 978-1-58246-394-0 (Gibraltar lib. bdg.)
Printed in China

Design by Katy Brown
Typeset in Kennerly
The illustrations in this book were rendered in watercolors.

1 2 3 4 5 6 – 15 14 13 12 11

First Edition

shine
shine

Buglette was a tidy little bug.

During the day, she often sang
as she scrubbed and swept.

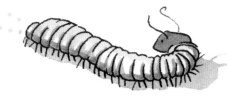

In the evening, she loved
to arrange her blankets.

After Papa Bug read books

and poured one last cup of water,

Buglette would settle neatly into bed.

But during the night . . . well, that was a different story.

Buglette had dreams.
BIG dreams.
And in the morning . . .

Buglette woke to a most untidy bed. Mama Bug shook her head and said, "Why can't you be more like Spot and Red? Such neat little sleepers."

"But Mama, I was building the tallest mountain ever!" said Buglette.

The next night, Buglette swung through the air.

And the night after that, she kicked a ball high into the sky.

In the morning, Buglette's pillow teetered overhead.

"Mama, I kicked a ball over the moon!" exclaimed Buglette.

Mama Bug sighed. "I just don't know how we ended up with a messy sleeper. Must have come from your father's side of the family."

That afternoon, the family picked aphids for dinner.

"Really, Buglette, what if your messy sleeping wakes the crow one of these nights?" asked Mama Bug.

The thought of the crow made Spot and Red tremble. That's when they decided to put a lid on Buglette's messy sleeping.

Push. Pull. Hoist. The acorn cap was a perfect fit.

Everything was peaceful.

But then, in her dream,
Buglette jumped from a plane.

She tossed and turned and thrashed about.
Bump! She kicked the acorn cap. As it fell to
the ground, it thumped Spot on the head.

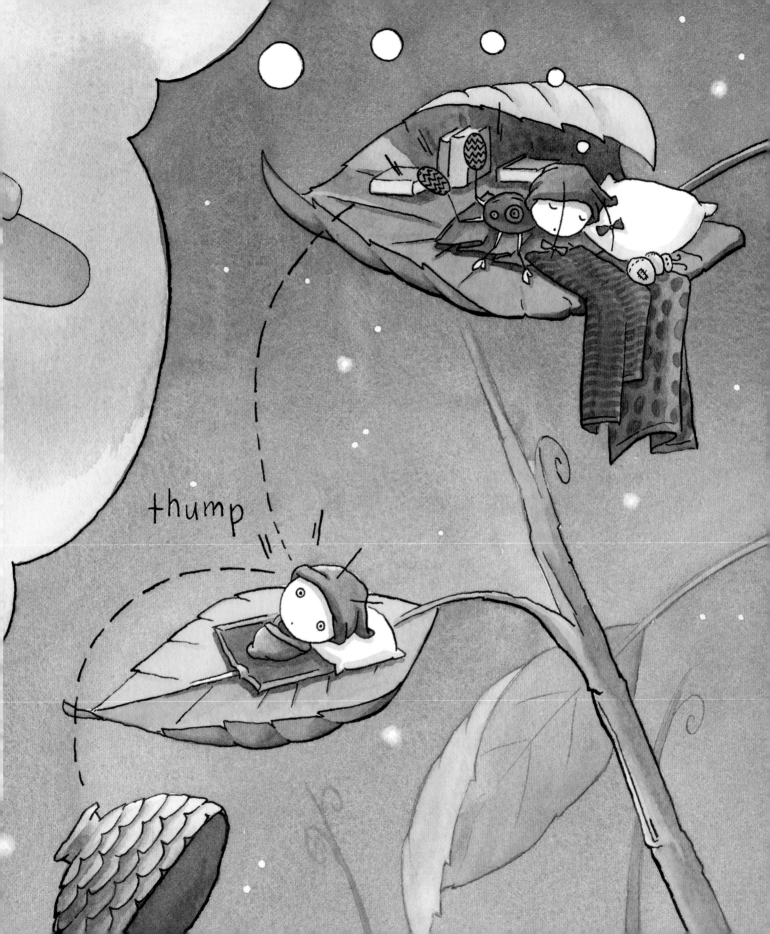

Spot's shout echoed through the stillness.

Wings flapped, and the crow landed.
The tiny bugs froze. *Step. Step. Step.*
The crow moved closer. When he
raised his beak toward Spot . . .

Buglette grabbed her blankets and
sailed bravely through the moonlight,
just as she had done in her dream.

Little Buglette
cast a **BIG** shadow,
and the crow paused.

Then Buglette threw a
blanket over the bird's eyes.